I0631154

Lights Out And Cry

SARAH A. HOYT

GOLDPORT PRESS

Copyright ©2023 by Sarah A. Hoyt

Cover copyright ©2023 by Sarah A. Hoyt

All rights reserved.

No portion of this book may be reproduced in any form without written permission from the publisher or author, except as permitted by U.S. copyright law.

To the memory of Lin Wicklund, who insisted Kyrie and Tom's child would be a kitteh-dragon.

Thank You

To my copy editor Sarah C. and dedicated beta Amy B. for proofreading above and beyond the call of duty.

Contents

Lights Out and Cry

NEW YEAR'S EVE. WHAT a perfect waste of a good night.

When you've lived even half the time I have, you come to realize all these years and other time demarcations of the apes are a nuisance.

They pat themselves on the back and congratulate themselves on surviving a few hundred days, and party wildly while they proclaim a new beginning.

It never is, because they're the same sad stinking apes they've always been.

And I want to make it very clear here: even shifters are apes, before enough time has passed that they've knocked the mud of mortality off their minds, and realized the apes don't matter.

A few of them have never knocked the mud off.

Which is why I was here in Goldport, on the slopes of the Rocky Mountains, as the year came to an end and a new year began in the time of Ragnarök.

It was cold enough to freeze my tail off, and I'd called a convocation of my minions.

You could hear them howling and growling here and there around the city, but it was barely audible through the sirens and the music and the occasional all too human shouting.

If I'd remembered this was supposed to be New Year's, even I'd have called the convocation elsewhere, not in the center of downtown. But it had seemed like such a good idea, so no one would get lost.

And here we were.

Downtown Goldport, in minus whatever weather, with a light coating of snow flakes falling. There was a bandstand with...I guess you could call them musicians. The group of six young men had the clothes and the instruments, the attitude and the hair, but really, their music was worse than some I'd heard in caves, played on rocks and bones than they could even imagine millennia ago.

And then there was the mayor. Middle-aged, balding, with a beautiful blond wife by his side, glad-handing and posing for the cameras as he wished everyone a Rocky Mountain High New Year.

And then—

And then there was a boom, a flash of light, and where the mayor had stood, there was a pile of flaming debris.

Everything was going according to plan. Soon, myself and my minions would have everything we needed to upend this sorry state of affairs for shifters, where they were subordinate to the apes.

Soon.

I wondered if the New Dragon would get in our way.

Tom had been working for over twelve hours. He'd insisted Kyrie sleep longer, so she'd only come in at just before midnight. And he was worried about that, as it was.

Though she said if working on her feet for twelve hours got the kid out, she was fine with it. There was a definite sense that she would like to get rid of the tenant in her belly. There had been dark mutterings about the baby using her bladder as a soccer ball, or tap-dancing on her lungs. He was turned and ready to come out, but didn't seem to really be in any hurry.

Tom flipped the burgers on the grill, plated eggs and bacon, and turned to put them on the counter for the servers to pick up. While looking that way, he tracked Kyrie in the crowd. She was talking to a table with a family of regulars, and they were all smiling and laughing with her. Kyrie had that ability. She made people feel as if the diner were home.

As he turned, a voice in his head spoke: *Son, there is something very wrong.*

It would be easier if the voice in his head were his father. In fact, his father was somewhere out partying with a girlfriend who was younger than Tom himself. And the idea of mystically speaking to his son in thoughts would probably make Edward Ormson laugh.

No, the voice in his head came with a feel of silk and ancient manners. It was the voice of the Great Sky Dragon, a Chinese quasi-divinity who turned out to be very much real and alive and ran the Three Luck Dragon, a restaurant at the edge of Goldport, Colorado.

Which would be almost funny, except why shouldn't he run his world empire from there? It was as good as anywhere else, and less likely to be noticed than in China. Probably. Tom had never asked the Great Sky Dragon when he'd made it to the United States, or why.

In some ways, considering the dragon organization was a criminal triad, you'd think a communist regime was custom-made for it. What was easier than hiding corruption in the corruption?

On the other hand, the Great Sky Dragon didn't think of his organization as corrupt, just as a tribe trying to look out for its kind.

And in neolithic terms, he was probably not corrupt at all.

As for why he considered Tom his son... Well, Tom was his only male descendant who shape-shifted into a dragon, even if the coupling that had given Tom his origin was lost in the mists of time, and Tom doubted anyone sequencing his DNA would find much of the Old Sky Bastard in it.

Tom turned back towards the grill and plated more food, ringing the little bell on the counter to alert his servers to its being ready. Mentally he said, *You know it's supposed to be a Greek choir, right, not a Chinese one?*

Choir? the voice in his mind asked.

And even though Tom knew it was actually impossible for the Great Sky Dragon to be that naïve about the civilization of the West, which he'd surely watched for millenia, Tom sighed and said, *Never mind. What is the great evil heading for us now?*

The gnawer in the dark. The enemy of mankind. He's found purchase in the minds of many of our kind, in town. They're everywhere. Trust nobody.

That...sounds pleasant. By our kind, you mean dragons?

No. All shifters. He's used his cursed ice to enslave many of them. And he seeks to make Ragnarök burn. Beware the bird and the ice.

Like that, the voice was gone, and Tom sighed again. Honestly, Greek choruses were more understandable. This was more like getting messages from the I-ching. Which the Great Sky Bastard had probably written. He was old enough.

He sighed deeply, turning towards the grill and the fire, muttering under his breath. "The superior man minds the burgers, and tends the fryer so it does not explode. And lets Ragnarök take care of its own bad Norse self."

THE LAST THING RAFIEL wanted to do was wait in line to enter the diner.

It had been so long since he'd been out partying—as a civilian—on New Year's Eve, that he'd forgotten the line out the door and around the block to get into the George for breakfast, even now at close to ten in the morning of the first of the year.

It was consistently one of the best days of the year for Kyrie and Tom. It had even been great for the former owner of the diner, before Kyrie and Tom. From what Rafiel understood from talking to Tom, business started running hot at the George at six pm or thereabout on the last day of the year, and it didn't quit till the evening of the first.

The crowds of people who came to eat dinner at the George on the last night of the year, and the staid neighborhood couples who stayed for the countdown—because it wasn't like they were going to a party, anyway—slowly gave way to revelers coming in for some food to cut all the liquor drunk shortly after midnight. And by four in the morning, the breakfast rush started, and on the first day of any given year, it didn't end till the dinner rush.

The line out the door and down a block from the George to the door of the headshop was the usual assemblage of college students and middle-aged couples, some of them still wearing funny hats, and the most die-hard still blowing on whistles that unrolled like shiny foil tongues and emitted a defiant "phooey."

It was interesting that, as far as he could tell, all the talk in line was about the parties they'd attended or their friends who'd gotten wasted, and not a single word was about the fact that the mayor had exploded on camera.

Sure, the mayor had been bizarrely murdered in the middle of Goldport at two minutes to midnight, but party on, dude. He'd been walking forward, slowly, with the line, and was now almost in front of the George. He could cut in line and go in to talk to Tom, but it would only cause protests and trouble.

Three college men ahead of him were discussing... Well, Rafiel had absolutely no idea what they were discussing. Probably women, as there were some female names mentioned, but Rafiel couldn't think straight enough to follow the conversation, because in the cold, clear morning, there was a smell of charred meat wafting over the crowd. It wasn't entirely abnormal, considering they were outside a diner and all. But after seeing the roast pieces of mayor, and spending most of the last ten hours helping photograph, tag and bag them, the smell stung the back of Rafiel's throat, and there would be very little needed to make him throw up.

He inclined his head, closed his eyes, and there, behind his eyes were thought-voices: *Boss? Boss? Boss?* And a sense of pressure. A sense of need.

To be fair, they weren't words, and they weren't really voices, but they had the feeling of someone calling him, the feeling of intense and needy requests for attention.

It was like...being surrounded by inquisitive toddlers pulling at your clothes and trying to get your attention. *What are you doing? Hey, look at me. Help me, now. We, the lion clan, need you.*

It had been a week, and Rafiel still wasn't used to this. He was used to questions from the chief of police or other investigators in the department, but not inside the space behind his eyes. That used to be private, and this intrusion was something new.

And he was used to being an investigator among equals, not the boss. For his sins, he seemed to be the new boss of the lion clan. He didn't know how Tom endured the whole leadership of the dragon clan, as well as control over every other clan.

Tom kept saying he was not and could not be the boss dragon, because he didn't want to be in charge of the mostly criminal operations of dragon shifters throughout the world.

Having heard all he wanted—and quite a bit he didn't—about the leadership, the kraal, of the previous boss of lions and his second-in-command, Rafiel was fairly sure that lion shifters were not any more morally pure than dragon shifters.

And Rafiel also didn't want any part of it. He'd only fought for the top spot because the alternative was dying. And he had strong objections to dying in his early twenties. For one, it would upset his mother. For another, it would upset his fiancée, Bea. And since Bea was a dragon shifter, there was a non-trivial chance she could set the world on fire.

So as much as he didn't want to be boss lion, it had to be dealt with somehow. As he had told his father, Rafiel had always thought it was his job and objective to bring law to shifters. And though his father had smiled, as though Rafiel had said he meant to change the world, Rafiel was deathly serious.

Most of what was wrong with the societies of shifters was that they thought themselves above humans and above the law, and killed and tortured and held protracted feuds both among themselves and innocent human bystanders, with no fear of authority and no written code they could refer to. Which meant the strong oppressed the weak, and the only justice was mob justice.

He would have to deal with his responsibilities to the lions at some point. And he'd have to figure out how much control Tom had over him, and what to do about it. There had been whispers that the power the dragons held had been stealthily or illegally acquired, and maybe that was it. Or maybe it was stupid tribal bullshit, of which he also didn't want any.

But— He pushed the intrusive not-quite voices to the back of his head. But, right now, he had other things to deal with. Like the exploding mayor.

The primacy of the clan would require a long discussion with Tom, and it would also require that Tom hadn't killed the mayor. On his own or by proxy.

Another waft of delicious grilled meat blew over the crowd, and Rafiel lost control. He barely managed to get out of line, and lean against a pole before he lost the contents of his stomach.

It wasn't much, as he hadn't eaten anything since dinner at his parents' home the night before, but the laughter and comments of, "Whoa, dude. Drank a lot last night?" didn't help.

He spat to clear the taste from his mouth and glared at the idiots in line, who somehow must have caught the danger they were in, because they stepped back. He dabbed at his mouth with Kleenex from his pocket and thought, *Right. This is stupid. Sure, cutting in line will make everyone furious. I'll go around the back. Why didn't I think of that? I need more sleep.*

Which was when his phone rang.

TOM, FRANKLY, COULD HAVE done with just one New Year's Eve off, or perhaps just enough time off to kiss his wife at midnight. But while he was behind the counter, turning out order after order, Kyrie his wife of less than a week and co-owner of the diner was circulating from table to table, taking orders, giving coffee warmups, setting plates down, smiling at all the regulars, and the many who would become regulars after today.

They had other regular employees on duty, including Conan, once an enemy and now a friend, a youngster whose Asian origin belied his fascination with and talent for Country music, and his fiancée, Rya, petite, brown-haired and a fox shifter, but the thing was, with all that, Kyrie and, of course, Anthony were the best and fastest of the servers. Kyrie, in particular, seemed to know everyone who came into the George, their diner in downtown Goldport, Colorado. And since their wedding, people would slip her envelopes of cash. Those who made the George part of their lives, whether it be for most of their meals, or a meal a week, or even a meal a month, would hear of the wedding, and would hand Kyrie a check. "For the baby." Or, "To start you guys right." Or, "You know, newlyweds always need something."

It always made Tom feel guilty. He could not explain they really didn't need it, not since the Great Sky Dragon had given him a check for more than he expected to make in the next fifty years or so. Because, first, how could he explain the Great Sky Dragon? Telling people he was sort of a Chinese god wouldn't explain what he had to do with Goldport. Second, how could he explain having gotten the money? He wasn't Chinese; he didn't look Chinese. He certainly didn't want to be the leader of all living dragons. At least, hopefully only living ones. Tom chased the thought of also commanding ghost dragons away. He still wasn't sure how an ancestor so many times distant that Tom probably had no traceable DNA of his left had gifted him with the curse and blessing of being a dragon shifter, much less the leader of them all. And some days, he wished someone else had gotten it.

Only if that had happened, there was a good chance Tom would never have met, much less married Kyrie.

He flipped a burger, removed a batch of fries, and heard a panicked whisper from the counter. "Tom, have you checked on Kyrie?"

"What?" he asked, turning half around. It was Rya, leaning over the counter. "Checked on her?"

"She went into the bathroom fifteen minutes ago. I'm covering her tables, but is she all right?"

Tom felt his eyes widen and commanded himself not to panic.

After all, Kyrie had been on her feet pretty much nonstop for twelve hours. That meant, if recent concerns were any indication, that her feet and ankles would be swollen, and she probably was dying for some time alone.

The thing was, why the bathroom? Though it was entirely possible she was asleep while sitting on the toilet, if that's what she'd intended to do, it was more likely she'd go into one of the storage rooms.

Or she could have gone into labor. If she had, wouldn't she have called him? On the other hand, Kyrie had a tendency to leave her phone under the counter when she was working the tables. He checked. Yep. There was her phone.

Kyrie wasn't due for another week, but their Nurse Practitioner, a member of the shifter community—her husband being a were-bear—had told them it was never exactly on time.

Tom had hoped Kyrie would not give birth till their friend could come back, because Kyrie would rather be attended by her than by the obstetrician she worked for, who was not a shifter. But that, too, was not under their control.

He looked around the diner till he spotted Anthony just delivering several plates of souvlaki to a table. He motioned urgently for Anthony to approach. Anthony stopped by a table and talked to the young man occupying it: Jason Cordova, also a were-bear, and an occasional server at the George. Jason looked up and towards Tom.

After years of managing the diner in times and conditions where no one would be able to hear him if he tried, because the background noise of the diner was such, Tom had become expert at communicating with his servers through nods and head movements.

Jason's look clearly was, "Need me, boss?" Tom nodded and pointed to the portion of the counter where they kept the server sign-up sheet. Jason got up, but Anthony beat him to the counter.

"Tom?"

"Could you take over the cooking?" Tom asked. He suppressed a wish to tell Anthony to keep a close eye on the fryer, the most expensive piece of equipment they owned, and one Tom was sure was only awaiting its opportunity to blow up. He lowered his voice. "Rya says Kyrie has been in the bathroom for fifteen minutes. I'd like to check on her. And she probably shouldn't be on her feet so much."

Anthony nodded. Jason was signing in as Tom lifted the part of the counter next to the sign-in and said, "Ask Anthony what tables he had." Then Tom trotted around the corner, past the salad mixing station, and into the long, slightly curving corridor, from which bathrooms opened on the right and storage rooms on the left. There was a line of women waiting for the bathroom, some looking very grumpy in the grey light from the glass door at the back. Tom stopped outside the women's bathroom and knocked. "Kyrie?"

For a long time, there was no answer. The women in line behind him chattered excitedly, as if they were watching a show.

He started positioning himself to take his shoulder to the door when there was a scrabbling on the other side, as though someone were having trouble getting hold of the handle.

Normally he'd wonder if Kyrie had shifted, mostly because as a black panther, she would have no thumbs, which made things like door handles difficult.

But Kyrie couldn't shift. Pregnant shifters didn't shift. Whichever form they got pregnant in, that was it until the the baby was out.

Unless Kyrie had given birth and— No. He wasn't going to think of it. Not at all.

"Kyrie?"

The door opened, and Kyrie's—fortunately human—face peeked out at him.

Kyrie was beautiful. Tom had moments of wondering how someone utterly ordinary-looking like him could have ended up with someone like Kyrie: golden skin and dark eyes, and curves in all the right places, even if at the moment those curves included a rounded belly. Or perhaps even more beautiful because of that curve. After all, it was his baby, proof that she favored him above all other men of their acquaintance.

Except right then, her face was pale, and she was scrunching it.

"Are you okay?" Tom asked.

She shook her head, and inhaled sharply.

Tom's eyes widened and he felt suddenly shaky. He had faced other dragons, massed, while he was alone. He'd fought all kinds of horrors, in all kinds of places. But now, his stomach fell and he felt as though he'd gone hollow.

He could have faced danger to himself at any time. But danger to his wife, danger to Kyrie, and a danger he could do nothing to mitigate? That made him both scared and powerless. "Kyrie, is it—"

She took a deep breath. "I was hoping it was nothing, but my water just broke. Could you get me a dry pair of pants? We need to go to the hospital."

Tom nodded. "I'll be right back."

He went back past the waiting women, who now sounded exhilarated, only to find he had trouble controlling his hands enough open the door to the storage room with his key.

Kyrie's parents! He needed to call Aurelia and Peter. They might have, through no fault of their own, missed most of their daughter's life, but they were trying to move to town, and they wanted to be part of her life now. And birth was important. Their grandchild was important.

Also, to be honest, he needed emotional support.

It was rare for births to have serious complications these days. And Aurelia, Kyrie's mom, said that most shifters were fine giving birth in the hospital. But most wasn't all, and with their...difference from normal, they were in unknown territory.

He said a prayer under his breath and plunged into the storage room, where they kept bins of thriftstore-bought clothes, clean and carefully folded for when they or any of their friends needed a change of clothes after a shift.

This was a different reason, of course, but they would serve.

"O FFICER TRALL?"

Rafiel, standing in the packed back parking lot of the George, near the dumpster no longer haunted by old Joe, the now-deceased alligator shifter, frowned at his phone. "Yes, Mr. Milagros?" he asked the chief of police.

Why "Mr. Milagros"? Why not "Chief?" Or "Boss," or "sir," or anything else? Mr. Milagros's chosen form of being addressed seemed like a reverse kind of populism, like he was reveling in not using titles and being one of the police officers.

Except he wasn't, of course. He was a retired police chief from LA who had no idea what policing really entailed in a small town in the Rockies, much less a small town as shifter-infested as Goldport. He kept thinking everything was big-city problems, and saw gangs around every corner. While the town might have a slight triad problem, what made it a problem was the fact that the triads were dragon shifters, not that they were a Chinese gang, per se.

But the mayor had found a statute that required the town to have a police chief, and promptly handed the post to his old buddy from California.

Now that Rafiel thought about it, he wondered how much more the mayor had thrown his weight around in other ways. And who, besides the much overworked and tired-of-nonsense police force, might have a reason to end the mayor?

It bore looking into, if all his appointees were as clueless as Mr. Milagros.

Milagros made a sound like blowing his nose, then said in a thickened voice, "Have you found out who killed Carl?'

Rafiel rolled his eyes up so far that he noticed the sky was opaque and grey-white with that look like it was about to snow.

And also that, almost straight over him, there was a dragon coming in for a landing. He looked up for a moment, trying to figure out who it was. But it wasn't Tom, or Conan, and it definitely was not the Great Sky Dragon.

Dragon-landing in the parking lot of a dragon-owned diner should be a non-event and a day ending in Y, but it didn't feel that way. Rafiel had, to put it in song terms, the feeling of "a bad moon rising." He opened the door to the diner and went into the back corridor.

Sure, this was the George and the middle of the day, but the way things had been this last week, he wasn't about to make any bets that the dragon wasn't coming down with the express intent of making lion-flambé.

First thing he noticed was a line of women waiting for the bathroom, which was par for the course for New Year's Day.

Inside, he said, "Well, sir, it's been about seven hours and we're still investigating." The dragon didn't land, or at least didn't land where Rafiel could see him. That was interesting.

"You know that if it's more than twelve hours, it's unlikely you'll catch whoever did it. Have you looked into bomb makers? That type of explosion and fire had to be some kind of substance we can track."

"We're...making inquiries," Rafiel said. Internally, he thought *A dragon is far more likely than C-4.*

"Well, I want a report on everything you're doing," Milagros rumbled, seemingly having forgotten to be mournful under his need to micromanage.

"Sir, that will only delay us," Rafiel said, and pushed off before *Mister Milagros* could put in another word.

And almost got run down by Kyrie and Tom. Kyrie was holding her midriff and leaning heavily on Tom.

"Out of the way," Tom said, and there was a weird boom behind his voice, which Rafiel had only heard when Tom was so disturbed he was about to call down the full dragon-leader persona with resonance from millennia ago and the full power of the Great Sky Dragon.

"My water broke," Kyrie said in an almost apologetic tone.

"I'll drive," Rafiel said. He spun around and opened the back door.

Tom didn't even argue, because argument required words. Instead, he made a sound that was something like between spitting and growling.

Rafiel said, "Come on. I can put the light on the roof!"

He loped ahead of Tom to open the door to the black SUV, and Tom helped Kyrie into the backseat. Rafiel removed the shoulder bag from Tom, getting another growl for his trouble—really, what was with Tom?—threw the bag onto the passenger seat, reached under for the lights, and stuck them atop the car, turned them on. Tom gave him a surprised look in the rearview mirror.

"What? I wasn't joking," Rafiel said. "It's faster. People get out of the way. Which hospital?"

"St. Gertrude's. On Sierra."

"Okay," Rafiel said, setting the GPS and taking off. He waited a couple of minutes, while Tom held Kyrie through a clenched-face contraction. "Tom, what do you know about the mayor?"

Kyrie frowned at Rafiel when he mentioned the mayor. It seemed to come out of nowhere. She took a deep breath and answered before Tom could. "Carl Graciano Phillips. He ran as an independent and surprised everyone by winning."

Rafiel gave her a curious look in the rearview mirror, and a smile. "How are you holding up? Any idea how far apart the contractions are? Because they will ask."

"Five minutes," Kyrie said. In the rearview mirror, Rafiel saw her eyes squeeze as she flinched through another contraction. "And my water broke ten minutes ago," she said, in a clenched-teeth way.

"Very well." Rafiel looked at Tom in the rearview mirror. "I have no idea what that means, but it seems like you're on top of it." Tom looked very nervous, but Rafiel would wager it wasn't any worse than the average first-time father waiting for birth. Well, and Tom's father's idea that between Kyrie and Tom, they were going to have a thing called a *kitty dragon* wasn't helping anyone, either. "Tom? Do you know of any dragons who have it in for the mayor?'

"What?" Tom's eyes went very large, and he stared at Rafiel with a look of complete incomprehension. "Is that why you offered to bring us to the hospital?"

"No, I offered to bring you to the hospital, because I have the siren." Rafiel pointed at the ceiling and drove down the street where cars got out of his way as fast as they could. "I love my siren, and I rarely get to use it. Sure, I could put it up there and turn it on when there are fresh doughnuts at the doughnut shop, but people tend to get upset. So I get to turn it on now. And can get you there fast. But I'd come to the diner to ask you if any of the dragons had a problem with Carl Graciano Phillips." And that was a heck of a mouthful of a name. How had the mayor come by it?

"Not that I know of," Tom said. He looked puzzled. "I have been working since yesterday at nine pm, you know? It's New Year's. I have no idea what happened to the mayor. I take it something happened?"

"You didn't have the TV on with the downtown New Year's celebration?" Rafiel pulled into the entrance of the hospital marked Emergency. There were cars in the way, but the siren worked its magic as even other cars in line tried to move out. In the end, Rafiel killed the siren and pulled near enough to the entrance.

"No," Tom said. He opened the door and waited while Kyrie flinched through yet another contraction. "I had New York City on. It's what the people expect. And they do a late midnight for Mountain time."

"Ah." Rafiel got the bag and helped Tom lead Kyrie into the reception, both of them supporting her through a silent, clenched-teeth contraction episode. "It's just that the mayor was...well. He exploded." He swallowed bile. "I... There were bits of charred mayor everywhere."

"I see why you'd think it had something to do with dragons, I suppose," Tom said. "I mean, fire. But the only way he would explode from being flamed would be if he had swallowed a stick of dynamite."

The thought hit Rafiel as true and also as hilarious. After all, who swallowed dynamite? Why hadn't he thought about that before? Oh, yeah, because he was running on no sleep.

And then they were in the reception area, getting Kyrie checked in, and the nurse was confused about which of them was her husband. They explained, smiling, and then Kyrie was in a wheelchair being wheeled back, and Tom grabbed Rafiel's arm, and spoke at a low volume. "Did he smell like a shifter?"

"The mayor? Kind of. So did his wife. But it was hard to tell by the time I got there. Mostly he smelled like roast meat."

Tom made a face. He had a hand in Kyrie's. "I'll ask around. I can't promise anything, but I'll ask around. The Great Sky Bastard was mind-talking me. I... I'll ask around."

Walking away, Rafiel wondered precisely what that meant. Was Tom going to physically call people and ask questions, or was this something more esoteric, having to do with mind-contact? Probably mind-contact. After all, Kyrie was giving birth.

By tradition, Tom was supposed to be capable of reaching into the mind of every shifter.

Rafiel didn't want to think about any of that too hard, partly because he and Tom were friends.

Tom and Kyrie were the first other shifters that Rafiel had met, knowing they were shifters, and the people he'd counted on through thick and thin, and would trust when his back was to the wall, and he couldn't trust anyone else.

They'd been through harrowing adventures together, and indeed, he wasn't sure he owed anyone—his fiancée Bea Ryu excepted—higher loyalty.

But he'd heard rumors over the last month that the dragons had usurped the power of the other clans of shifters, and that the lion shifters, in particular, had once been the top clan.

He wasn't sure if he believed any of it. The sources were confused, and frankly despicable. But here was the thing: they were also in Rafiel's head.

Since killing his rival to the leadership of the cat clan—it was more than lions—he'd found that he dreamed of lives and places where he'd never been. Dreams of Africa and the Savannah were pretty common, but so were dreams of hunting. And in those dreams, normal humans were just prey.

And in those dreams, in the dark of night, a voice came and talked.

He wasn't sure whose voice it was. But he knew two things: it was immensely ancient, and it was relentless. Okay, three things: he knew he'd have hated this being in person, if he ever met him.

He didn't know if Tom had the same dreams, nor what his powers as de facto dragon leader were. But he hoped they weren't as crazy as Rafiel's own.

Rafiel sighed, watching the wheelchair with Kyrie vanish down the hallway, Tom by her side, and turned to find a nurse smiling at him. She was maybe in her thirties, blond, and very pretty. It seemed to him she smelled of shifter, but then again, his nose had been full of charred meat smell for hours. He rubbed it with the back of his hand. "How long will it take? I mean...the birth?"

"Oh, could be a couple of hours or most of a day," she said with a smile. "Family?"

Rafiel almost said, "No, friends." But what the heck. Actually, for sure, seemingly he and Kyrie were related. Because the lion-panther gene ran through only part of the clan, and they were related. Just very far off. "Cousins," he said. "I mean, we're friends, too." He gave the nurse a nervous smile. "I'll call and see how it's going."

He was walking to the door back to his car when his phone rang. It would be Milagros.

K YRIE HATED HOSPITALS. SHE had always hated hospitals, from their smell to the impersonal bullying. It was like doctors and nurses didn't know how to do anything without bullying the patients, and bullying was their normal mode of getting through the day.

They told you what to do in a manner that made you feel vaguely guilty and evil for disobeying. Except Kyrie then felt guilty for obeying, too. Fortunately, being a shifter meant that you didn't spend much time in hospitals. You healed very fast, and you could usually hide an injury long enough.

But when you were in hospitals—for Kyrie, twice, one after a bad car accident with a foster family—you were on edge the whole time, because you could smell blood and sick humans, which of course caused the hunting instincts of your shifter form to be on high alert.

The pain wasn't helping, either.

Then there was the room. The bed was molded all in plastic, like one of the cheapest forms of kiddy toy furniture, and on it was a mattress that was obviously a single piece of foam rubber. It might very well have been extremely hygienic, but it was also very uncomfortable.

And Tom was fussing, which Kyrie supposed was perfectly normal for a new father. Or an almost-new father.

He stood by the bed while the nurses made Kyrie look comfortable, while she really wasn't. She'd changed into the hospital gown that wouldn't really cover anything and was lying splayed while the nurse looked.

Then the door opened, and a young man came in. A very young man. Six-foot-four, a substantial portion of his ancestry from the African continent, shoulder-length hair in a ponytail, but with a pretty face that looked barely past adolescence. At a glance, she thought he'd be about seventeen, but he was wearing scrubs and smiled at her, a wide smile. "Hi, I'm Doctor Henry. I know you were hoping to have your nurse practitioner deliver or Doctor Richards, but they're both off and she left me all the notes while she's out of town. We often work together. Okay if I take a look?"

She grinned at him despite herself, then flinched for the space of a contraction. He was really incredibly young-looking to be a doctor, but he looked so kind.

Dr. Henry looked under the gown, and the blanket decorously draped over her lap. Kyrie thought with some frustration that the entire arrangement seemed designed to keep her from seeing what was going on, and everything felt kind of weird just then. The obstetrician smiled up at her over the blanket on her knees.

"Two centimeters," he said. "Moving right along."

"So," Kyrie said, "it will be soon?"

The young doctor grinned "Well. No. I mean, we don't know. First children are always a bit of a gamble. So probably a few hours. Don't worry. Chances are it will be perfectly okay. We'll be by to check on you. And we'll come if you ring the bell." He hesitated, at the foot of the bed. "We obviously didn't have your birth plan. You...don 't want painkillers?"

"No," Kyrie said, aware she probably sounded like some kind of earth mother. She really would have preferred to be zonked out of her head. If the initial contractions were any indication, this was going to be a whole lot of no fun.

However, the reason she hadn't been planning to come to the hospital at all was that she was afraid to shift into a panther right after giving birth.

A panther rampaging through a hospital was bad, but a drugged out-of-her-mind panther rampaging through the hospital would be worse.

"If you change your mind, let us know." And that is when she caught it... The shifter smell. Well, at least that was something. If she shifted into a panther, the doctor wasn't going to be horrified and run away screaming.

But it reminded Kyrie that she'd promised to tell her parents when she was in labor. Her phone had stayed in the pocket of her jeans, which were neatly folded over a chair out of her reach

"Tom, "she said, and realized he was on the phone. "Are you calling my parents?"

But he shook his head and turned away from her and walked toward the door, hunching his shoulder as if to protect the screen from her.

Words drifted back to her. "A dragon what?"

R AFIEL GRABBED THE PHONE as he got in the car. "Yes, Mr. Milagros?"

"Any breakthroughs?"

"Not yet, sir, but I'm pursuing leads."

"It's been over twelve—"

"Hours. Yes, I know, sir."

Milagros huffed. "Murder by explosive is bound to have left a trail. I mean, where did the explosive come from, and how was it thrown at the mayor?"

But Rafiel remembered the pieces of mayor all over. Itty bitty pieces. Like he'd exploded from the inside out. He had a wild impulse to ask

Mr. Milagros if the mayor had been on nytroglycerin for his heart, but he suppressed it. He was rebellious, not stupid.

"And what are Frick and Frack doing, anyway?" Mister Milagros asked.

"Sir?"

"The cousins!"

"Oh. Officer Wolfe and Officer Nickopoulous?" Rafial asked, being exceedingly correct.

Another huff. "Yes. Them. What are they doing?"

"They're following leads, sir. You might wish to call them." And then he hung up.

Cas and Nick were going to kill him. They were going to outright murderize him. But if it got Mr. Milagros off his hair, he couldn't say he was even sorry.

Cas and Nick were indeed cousins and officers of the Goldport police force.

They were also werewolves. But it occurred to Rafiel that he actually had no idea what those two were doing.

Their ideas ranged from inspired to insane.

Thing was, this being Goldport, there was no actual guarantee that the insane ideas wouldn't pay off.

Some years ago, a variety of shifter beetles who laid their eggs in shifter corpses had spread shifter-attracting pheromones around downtown.

Since then, shifters had been coming to Goldport through every possible means: they left the highway, they stopped off on bus trips, they wandered out of airports during a layover. There might actually be more shifters than normal people in town. There was no actual way to tell.

But thinking about Cas and Nick gave Rafiel ideas. The cousins came from a traditional shifter family from Greece.

For years, they'd managed to hide *from him* that they were shifters by using some kind of herbal tea their grandmother made.

So given that Cas and Nick came from a traditional culture, both being the first generation born in America, and since they had—presumably—family stories about this, they might be working on that knowledge, somehow. They might have some idea what caused the mayor to explode.

He dialed Cas, who answered with, "Yeah."

"Suppose the mayor was shifter."

Was it Rafiel's impression or was there a long silence before an answer? "Yeah?"

"You smelled shifter?"

Cas made a sound: it was a whistle that wasn't quite a whistle, just a letting out of air forcefully between his teeth. "Not...not in the incident, no...or from... Well, from the pieces."

"Oh?" Rafiel had known Cas a long time, and he could sort of hear what hadn't been said. "Before?"

"Uh uh." Cas sighed. "Look, yeah. I was part of the mayor and his wife's escort to an event last summer. And—uh... Yeah. They're both shifters. Well, he was. She presumably still is."

"So? What kind of shifter explodes?" Rafiel asked, not willing to let it go.

Another low whistle. Not an actual whistle, but again the sound of air escaping between teeth. "I don't know for sure. I mean, I can't tell you for sure. When I asked my grandma..."

"You asked your grandma?"

"Yeah, of course. Do I look stupid? I called her and asked."

Rafiel had the momentary irrelevant thought that he should ask Rafiel if it was in Greek or English, but really, it was none of his business. He'd never heard Cas speak Greek, not even to Nick, but he wouldn't be surprised at all if he heard him. Of course, he also had no idea where Cas's grandma lived. Could be on the other end of town. "So what did she say?"

"There are problems talking to Grandma about this stuff. For one, she's paranoid about mentioning any of it over the phone. She keeps talking about hunters. I gather she means shifter-hunters, though I can never get— She never told us precisely who she means. And then she's afraid the 'bad ones' will find her. Whoever the bad ones are."

"Okay," Rafiel said, disappointed. "So I gather you didn't find out anything?"

"I didn't say that. I don't think there is a word for it, or not a word she knew, but I gathered a sort of picture."

"Are you going to tell me?"

"Not over the phone." There was a long silence and a sigh. For some reason, Rafiel had the impression that Cas was frowning in the way he did when he had a headache coming on. "Look, yeah, Grandma is old country. It doesn't mean she's wrong. There is a feeling something is off. I don't like it. How about you meet me outside the morgue?"

"Uh?"

"Listen, Raf, just do it. I think Nick is on the phone with Milagros, and I'm going to need help."

"You are?" Rafiel was surprised at hearing himself called Raf. To his knowledge, neither of the cousins had ever called him that. No one had ever called him that, except his first girlfriend, long ago. But it came across as Cas being exasperated enough, he couldn't say the whole name.

He sounded exasperated as he said, "You have no idea."

This was absolutely true. And Rafiel wanted to reach through the phone and strangle Cas, or at least shake him till he talked. But the reaching-through the phone ability was still impossible. And he wanted to know. Stewing, he set the GPS for the city morgue. What the actual heck? Why the morgue? Was Cas expecting a zombie apocalypse?

TOM HAD CALLED THE diner, because, well, how could he not? Yeah, he trusted Anthony as much as he trusted himself behind the counter, but since he always expected the fryer to explode on him, he also expected it to explode on Anthony. So he'd called to check on Anthony.

Of course, it all went sideways from the moment his father answered the phone.

Tom's father, Edward Ormson, was... Well, he'd once been a big-time lawyer in New York City. He'd worked for the dragon triads. He'd been a pretty terrible father, too. Not that he was a bad person. It was more like he was a teen who'd never grown up, and couldn't understand why this child was impinging on his time or on what he wanted to do. That is, until he'd been reunited with Tom in Goldport, and reconciled to the fact that his son was a dragon. He loved Tom and Kyrie, and was enthusiastic about becoming a grandfather, which didn't prevent him from being involved—hot and heavy—with a twenty-year-old dragon shifter named Sandra. Tom had taken great care to stay out of Sandra's head. He wasn't a hundred percent sure how the whole thing worked, not even vaguely, but his ability to drop into other dragons' heads wasn't a hundred percent under his control. Except that— Well, except that he wouldn't drop into Sandra's, if he could absolutely help it. Because the idea of dropping in on her and his Dad in an intimate moment was enough to make sure he and Kyrie had no more kids, ever.

Having his dad answer the phone brightly with, "Hello, son," was a surprise, particularly since Tom had dialed the diner's landline. He'd presumed Edward was somewhere sleeping off the New Year's partying, but also because his dad being the one to come to the phone meant everyone was very busy. Okay, so it was the first of the year. Still. There would usually be a responsible adult who'd grab the phone before Edward did.

"Dad."

"Yeah, I came by and I'm pitching in." This wasn't as horrifying as it might be, since his father had proven to be a good fill-in for waiting at tables, even if he threw all of Tom's calculations off by refusing to take pay. "How is Kyrie?"

Tom gave a look to the bed. "She's fine. Or I think she's fine. The doctor said it will be a few hours. Probably."

"That's what I figured, so I thought I'd help a bit around here first before heading to the hospital. I called your in-laws, by the way. They're heading in."

"Thank you," Tom said. And hesitated. Of course, he had only called out of habit of keeping an eye on the diner. The diner had been his obligation these last two years, the first thing he thought of when waking up, and his last thought when going to bed. He didn't really have much time away from the diner, and whenever he did, he always worried about...everything. "Everything is fine there?" he asked, hesitantly. "I mean, enough people to attend at tables and all?"

"Yeah," his dad said. "Plenty of servers. It's starting to slack off a bit, but will probably restart in three hours or so when the dinner rush starts. And no, son, the fryer hasn't exploded."

Tom was trying to conjure a dismissive sound and a convincing way to say that he wasn't worrying about that in the least, when his father said, "The only thing that has gone wrong... Well, you're going to have to repair the ladies' restroom. We've shut the water off in there, and we put a sign on the door to make sure everyone knows the men's restroom is now unisex."

It was as though Tom's whole body clenched like a fist. "Why? What happened?"

"Well," his father said. "A dragon got in there and shifted."

"A dragon did what?"

His dad sighed. "First indication we had was water under the door. We called... Uh, I called Sandra, and her dad came in—"

Just lovely, considering that Sandra's dad was the Great Sky Bastard by one of the Great Sky Bastard's various concubines. "What did he do?"

"I don't know. He came in, in human form, with a few of his henchmen, and, well...he got the door open, and I presume he got the dragon out of there."

Or ate him, Tom thought. Either was actually possible.

"As you can imagine, the place was pretty trashed, though. Old Lung says that it wasn't one of his. I understand this was a Norse dragon. But he also said something about bad ice. And he thinks the dragon was after the three times precious. Since this isn't Lord of the Rings, I presume he was after the Pearl of Heaven. He was following traces or something?"

Well, that made perfect sense, because long ago, when Tom had first come to Goldport, he had kept the Pearl of Heaven—which he'd stolen out of a lot of misguided assumptions—inside the flush tank in the ladies' restroom at the George. That had been years ago, but he knew such things left a trace. "Does... Uh... Does Mr. Lung have the slightest idea why?"

"No," Edward said. "Not the slightest."

Tom frowned. He'd had the Pearl of Heaven handed to him last week. And the Great Sky Bastard had refused to accept it. Tom thought he'd hidden it well, but the problem was it would be unprotected. And if the Norse dragons were looking for it...

He hung up and turned around to see Kyrie pant and moan through a contraction. He was fairly sure he didn't teleport to her side, but he was there in a second, holding her hand. "It's all right, honey. It's all right," he said. It felt like she was about to break his hand, but he didn't complain. Hey, he was a shifter. He'd heal easily. As her face started to un-scrunch, he said, "My dad says he told your mom and dad, and they're on the way."

As he spoke, he heard noise in the hallway, and in the next minute his in-laws were in the room. They were the most ill-assorted couple as to appearance, probably explaining why, before she met them, Kyrie had been placed all over the ethnic and racial map by everyone who met her, from Mediterranean to Middle Eastern, to parts of Asia and everywhere in between.

Her mom was probably, she thought, half non-tribe specific African. Or to be exact, she was half-descended from the past leader of the lion clan, which was mostly, but not exclusively, African. And her father had been very African. He might very well have been born in Africa before humanity had lived anywhere else. Leaders of clans were usually that long-lived. If they didn't get killed in Ragnarök, of course. Her mom was anyone's guess. Kyrie's mom had never met her own mother, and had no idea what she'd looked like.

Aurelia looked like a darker, middle-aged Kyrie, according to Tom. The resemblance was particularly obvious in their voices and expressions. That Kyrie's mom was apparently big noise in the world of physics struck Tom as very funny, since he couldn't possibly imagine Kyrie doing something so divorced from looking after people.

Kyrie's father, meanwhile, was blond, blue-eyed, and looked like a middle-aged physics professor, which he in fact was.

And that was the thing. The couple looked incredibly ill-matched until they started talking and you realized they were both utter and complete geeks, and therefore completely well-matched. It wasn't just the physics thing. Those two got nostalgic and over-explainy talking about old movies, old books, and old comics, to the point they'd once cornered Conan and talked at him for three hours about the comic books that Conan's parents used to learn English, and after which he was named.

Poor Conan had sat there, being excruciatingly polite to his elders and looking like he was wondering if pretending death would allow him to escape, until Kyrie had taken pity on him and dropped into the conversation to remind him he had promised to sing that night. He hadn't, but his singing was always well-received and increased receipts in the diner, so he'd grabbed his guitar and perched on one of the barstools, crooning country western till Kyrie's parents left. Kyrie and Tom, perhaps unfairly, had been highly amused by how his desire to sing some more would intensify as soon as her parents looked in his direction between songs.

Not that Aurelia and Peter meant to bore anyone, of course. They were nice people, intense and knowledgeable and perhaps—due to the circumstances of their lives reinforcing their professional inclinations—slightly tone-deaf when it came to reading people.

Right then they swooped in, full of information, or as Tom would phrase it, *having read way too much.*

They smiled at him, but with a slightly confused look, as if they didn't quite realize what he could possibly have to do with the occasion, and Aurelia proceeded to adjust Kyrie's pillow, and help her straighten herself on the bed, and give her water, all the while babbling about effacing and cervix, and heaven alone knew what.

Freed for the moment from the grip of the bone-crushing handhold, Tom wondered if he should do something about the Pearl of Heaven.

When the Great Sky Dragon—to Tom, he'd always be that, as long as he lived, and...yeah, Tom understood that he himself had most of the powers associated with the job, but why should he have to admit it?—had refused to take back the artifact of power of the dragon clan, Tom had done what a sane dragon would do. He had shifted into a dragon, and on a cold, clear, winter night, had flown up to one of Colorado's mountain reservoirs, and put the pretty, dangerous thing under a lot of water.

Water, from what he understood, made the perception of the pearl dim out. In fact, he'd kept it hidden inside a toilet tank for months after he'd stolen it. A reservoir was bigger than a toilet tank and it had a hell of a lot more water. So it should be safe, and not call to any dragons around. But now he wondered. If someone had sensed, it in the bathroom years after...

Well, nothing he could do about it right now. And he couldn't imagine what difference it made, anyway. Supposedly, it had all the knowledge of the dragon clan, and granted full powers on the Great Sky Dragon.

The problem was that some millenia back, there had been a transference of power which seemed to have been botched, meaning that the Great Sky Dragon had inherited the pearl and the body of knowledge that the old alligator shifter known as Old Joe had called "the Dragon Egg," but not whatever the oral knowledge was supposed to be passed from Great Sky Dragon to Great Sky Dragon that allowed the knowledge in the Pearl of Heaven to be accessed and read.

In a way, for millennia now, like in some great dystopian science fiction novel, the leader of dragons had inherited the equivalent of a computer drive that he had no idea how to open, and displayed it, dramatically, as a symbol of leadership, while not being able to do anything for which it was designed.

He wondered if the Norse dragons and their newly awakened queen would know how to read the thing. But probably not. It seemed like the Pearl of Heaven was specifically Chinese. Then again, who knew? A horse shifter who claimed to be Loki had tried to steal the Pearl of Heaven of appease the Queen of Norse dragons, aka the Queen of the North.

The fact that the real Loki was a greasy, sidling disappointment, not at all like the movies or comics, just made it all worse.

"Tom!" It was Kyrie, and he again seemed to teleport to her side, holding her hand through a really bad contraction.

She took a deep breath once it had passed, and asked, "Maybe we should call the doctor? They're getting close. And really really bad."

"I'll go find a doctor," his father-in-law said, heading out of the room.

R AFIEL DROVE UP TO the morgue, a one-floor building on the outskirts of Goldport. There was no black SUV in the parking lot, but Cas was there.

Cas and Nick, raised together, more like brothers than cousins, had developed a hobby of rehabilitating old cars—often almost entirely rebuilding old cars rescued from junkyards or bought at auction—and each of them drove the newly-fixed car for a while, then sold it, and moved on to the next one.

This one was a 1950s Cadillac, in deep, glowing blue, a beautiful thing, all curves and jewel tones. There was no way anyone but Cas or Nick was driving one of those in a Colorado winter.

Rafiel pulled up next to it, and Cas reached over and opened the door. Right. They'd play it that way.

Rafiel slid into the passenger seat, and looked at Cas.

"I know it was you who got Mr. Milagros to call one of us in."

"I didn't mean to—"

"No, I know. He was probably driving you insane. He seems to have it in for you particularly, I'm not sure why. Anyway, the thing is, I sent Nick to him, and I came here, because I think things are about to get ugly, but I didn't know what to do... Now you're here, and while things might get ugly, at least there's two of us. Though it might not make much difference. But hey, at least someone will hear my screams when shit hits the fan."

"Okay, you're starting to scare me. Why are we at the morgue? And what's about to happen? Is there a zombie apocalypse about to happen?"

Cas shook his head. "Well, no. Probably not that." He frowned.

"Probably? The last time a corpse caused this much commotion you weren't involved. It was when those two crazy beetle shifters were filling up the grounds of the castle with their eggs in murder victims, and—" He saw the flinch, and the look in Cas's eyes, and grabbed Cas's wrist before he realized what he was doing. "What? Please, tell me this is not like that. Please?"

Cas shook his head. He extricated his arm from Rafiel's grasp, then, slowly, almost carefully, he put his head down, so his forehead touched the leather-covered steering wheel of the car. "Rafiel, I am not sure this is an exact translation, but the best I can understand, what my grandmother was talking about was the reproduction of a rare kind of shifter called the phoenix."

"What? The mayor was a phoenix?"

"Yeah. The mayor and, as far as I can tell, his wife. And the reproductive cycle of the phoenix is not precisely as has been represented."

"They don't catch fire?" Rafiel asked. "And burn up completely, leaving behind an egg?"

"Uh... Kind of. But not... There are very few phoenixes, and they don't reproduce often, which probably accounts for the confusion. Part of the reason there are very few phoenixes is that for them to be willing to reproduce at all means to be willing to die. If they're willing to let the process happen—and I don't know if it's volitional, or if it's just mating with another of their kind—they know that any moment, they might blow up and burn. From what Grandma said—and remember, Grandma is one of us, a shifter, which means...well, she once gave me the impression she remembered the Trojan war. Or more than one of those—in the old days, when a phoenix blew up and turned into a bunch of souvlaki, ready for the eating...well, a lot of creatures, mostly not shifters, came out of the woodwork to eat the buffet. Which means, of course, that very little was left. Maybe one piece, to become a new phoenix, and therefore it gave us the idea that the phoenix burned to be reborn."

"Wait, that's not true?"

"Oh, no. The phoenix reproduction cycle is far more interesting than that. You see..." Cas lifted his forehead from the steering wheel and sat up very straight, staring ahead into the parking lot of

Shorty's Drugs across the street. "When a mommy phoenix and a daddy phoenix love each other very, very much—"

"Cas, so help me, I'm going to hit you."

"Don't. This will have enough pain for both of us. Anyway, it seems like when they get together, their entire bodies get fertilized, and then they explode. And each little bit becomes—"

"Dear Lord."

"To put it mildly."

Rafiel looked, in some horror, towards the morgue building. "How long till the place is bursting with babies? And what do we do with all of them?"

"I don't know. A few hours, Grandma said... And I have no idea. I don't think there are that many foster families in Colorado."

"They are babies? Human babies? When they...emerge? Hatch? Whatever the heck they do?"

"Oh, yes. Normal appearance babies. Like most of us, they don't shift till adolescence. And when they do, they become a beautiful, glowing bird, nothing too scary. Though they are under the chicken clan."

"I've heard that the chickens are... I've heard they're dangerous—"

"Yeah. And you haven't heard Grandma. But these aren't chickens. They're phoenixes. And right now, they'll be babies. Hundreds of babies. I don't know how we're going to explain it."

"Nor how we're going to explain the murder to Mr. Milagros," Rafiel said. "Since he wasn't murdered, particularly."

"Nick said he would make up something," Cas said, and only the wary tension on his face and the way his eyes squinted gave away how much the prospect scared him.

"Push," Doctor Henry said, and Kyrie obeyed, until he screamed, "Stop pushing."

Kyrie growled at him, her eyes momentarily looking very much feline.

"Sorry," the young doctor said apologetically. He did something under the covering draped over Kyrie's knees. "Just making sure the shoulders can come out. Now push with the next contraction."

She obeyed. Pushing was easier than not pushing, which she figured made complete sense, since pushing would be the thing that would bring this kid out, right?

The contraction hit, and she pushed. The pain seemed like too much to be part of any normal process, but everyone told her things were proceeding normally, and she couldn't say it felt like she was pushing out a full-grown human being, not a baby.

All she knew for sure was that the pain was ten times worse if she wasn't touching Tom. So, she held on to Tom's hand, and squeezed hard as she pushed. As the pain receded, she realized that Tom looked pale as a sheet, and removed his hand, to shake it.

"Sorry, sorry," she said.

He grimaced, then smiled. "It's okay. I heal quickly."

"Okay," Dr. Henry said. "Push."

Kyrie grabbed blindly for Tom's arm.

"**O**KAY," RAFIEL SAID. "I say we go and deal with this."

"But what the hell are we going to do?"

"Well... We're going to deal with it. Whatever it is."

Cas hesitated. He took a deep breath. "All right," he said.

They opened the car doors at the same time, as though they'd co-ordinated it, which, of course, was when a car pulled into the parking lot.

It was a convertible, which was funny enough for January the first in light snow. But the funniest thing of all was that the woman inside was smoking hot.

No, not as in a spectacular look, but snow melted directly around her, and there was smoke rising from her head. It took Rafiel a moment to recognize the mayor's wife.

"**P**USH!"

There was feeling... Kyrie would never be able to describe it. It wasn't something she had ever felt before, and there didn't seem to be words for it. It was as though something internal had let go. Like...like something had been knotted up and suddenly cut loose.

And the pain stopped, like that, followed by a flood of relief.

"It's a boy!" Dr Henry proclaimed in a happy voice, like he came from a time before ultrasounds and Kyrie and Tom had been waiting for the one male heir to the kingdom. "A beautiful little boy."

Kyrie let go of Tom's hand and leaned back against the pillows, nerveless and exhausted.

She closed her eyes. Somewhere, down below her blanket-covered knees, someone was touching her, and there were discomforts and twinges of pain, but it was nothing as clear and defined as the pain she'd felt before. She took deep breaths and might have dozed until someone touched her shoulder. "Kyrie."

She opened her eyes. Tom was holding a little…well, a baby. Someone had cleaned the baby up and put a diaper on him. He was red, and wrinkled, and the most beautiful thing she'd ever seen.

He was also crying in a little, thin, high voice.

And Kyrie asked the most stupid question she'd ever asked in her entire life. "Is it ours?"

Tom laughed. It was a weird, pained laugh, almost a cough, followed by something like a hiccup, then a giggle. "No, hon. I just grabbed him as he was walking towards the hall, to the vending machines."

She scooted up, causing some protest from Dr Henry from under the blanket that sounded like, "Just a stitch."

And then… And then Tom was putting the baby in her arms.

"You know," Tom said from very far away, as she counted all the fingers and toes, having read somewhere that if a baby had ten fingers and ten toes, the rest was likely to be all right. "We never talked about what we were going to call him."

Which sounded insane, but happened to be true. They'd been so…involved in the baby and the reality of having a baby while running a diner and trying to plan a wedding, that they'd never come up with a name. They'd gone from calling the baby Blueberry, to calling him Shrimp, to calling him Bundle of Baby, or just Baby, without ever deciding on a name.

"We're not normal parents," Kyrie said on a groan, feeling completely inadequate for the task ahead, and knowing it was too late and that they were responsible for this small human for at least the next eighteen years. She took a deep breath, inhaling new-baby smell, and—

Oh no. She knew that tangy, almost spicy scent.

"Tom," she said, with some urgency. "Tom. Smell your son."

Tom inhaled. And his eyes went side.

They looked at each other in complete horror, realizing their little baby would grow up to be a shifter. Like them.

"MRS. PHILLIPS?" RAFIEL SAID, rushing up to her. She was wearing what she'd worn the night before, obviously an outfit designed to be captured on cameras. It was almost retro.

Fitted skirt and blouse, overtopped by a blue coat cut to display her slim waist. She wore a matching scarf tied over her blonde hair, and her makeup was impeccable.

The blue eyes in the middle of the carefully applied makeup were panicked.

"I must... There is something...my children."

Rafiel took a deep breath. He had a feeling any minute now there would be lightly roasted mayor's wife all over the parking lot. And damn it, he didn't want to do this. He didn't want to deal with this. "Of all the stupid ways to reproduce," he said. Ethically, he supposed it was better than beetles who laid eggs in the corpses of deceased shifters, but really.

Mrs. Phillips eyes went huge and round. A carefully manicured hand went to her throat. "You know!" she said.

"Of course I know," Rafiel said. His voice was little more than a growl. "I'm also a shifter."

"A phoenix?" the woman said, with sudden hope. What? She was hoping to— Was there a community of phoenix shifters somewhere? Did they raise babies by the batch load? They'd have to, wouldn't they?

"No. A lion. How close are you to—"

"Spawning? I don't know. He told us it wouldn't be for years. He lied."

"Um... Clearly. Who is he?"

"No time," she said. She shoved a sheaf of papers at him. "I was hoping to come across some of the spider monkeys. They'd— Well, there's a lot of them. If you call— Mr. Idon'tknowwhatyournameis— Officer! Take cover."

The smoke emanating from her was now so thick and choking he didn't need to be told twice, particularly since Cas was in wolf form and running hell for leather to hide behind his car across the parking lot.

Rafiel dived, rolled, and was almost completely behind his SUV when he heard the soft explosion. It was a weird sound. He hadn't been there for the mayor, but he'd heard that sound over and over in replays of the mayor's explosion on the TV recording. It was part of what had thrown them off, because it was such a soft, organic sound that it didn't match any explosive known to man.

The best way to explain it would be if someone had set off an explosion inside a roll of meat. Which, now that he thought about it, was precisely what had happened. Only more like every part of the mayor, and now his wife, was trying to get away from every other part.

He hunched close behind the car, arms over his head, while the mayor's wife rained down all around. When it stopped, he stood up and said a bunch of profoundly non-creative words, then realized Cas, in wolf form and naked except for his drawers dangling from one leg, was smelling one of the bits of mayor wife, and said, "Cas. No. Stop it."

Cas looked over his shoulder at Rafiel, slitted yellow eyes looking somehow both shocked and offended. In the next second, Cas was coughing, contorting, his body changing. Rafiel averted his eyes, as was only decent when another was changing shape. In moments, a naked Cas loped across the parking lot, grabbed underwear, sweat-pants and shirt from the ground where they'd fallen when he'd shifted suddenly. "At least they didn't tear," he said. Rafiel thought he was lucky, because he shifted into a relatively small shape that allowed him to shift without tearing clothes.

He looked around at Rafiel. "Now what? We already didn't know what to do before."

Rafiel sighed and bit his lower lip. "She said she was going to ask the spider monkeys." He was looking towards the door of the morgue. There would be someone there, right? If they were very lucky, it was just a guard, on the first day of the year, and he wasn't going to come out and see what was going on. If they were really very very lucky, no ambulance would pull in with a fresh stiff.

He closed his eyes and prayed in the general direction of a divinity for luck, because honestly, they needed luck like they'd never had before. The last thing he wanted to explain was how they'd come to be in a parking lot with flambéed wife of mayor.

"How are we supposed to call the spider monkeys? Are they in the phonebook under S?"

Rafiel shook his head. He'd realized some time ago that Cas tended to become very aggressive when he was cold. Or hungry. And he was probably both, having shifted to wolf and back again in the space of a few minutes.

"No," he said. "But Dr. Fleming is. And he's a vet, so he probably has an answering service who will call him if one of his clients has an emergency."

"Dr. F— Oh." Cas sighed. "The guy who went camel."

Some years ago, for reasons that Rafiel wasn't absolutely sure he'd ever understood, one of the local vets, who happened to be a camel shifter, had disappeared by the simple expedient of going to the zoo and assuming his camel form.

It wasn't, he'd come to find, really rare for shifters. It might be the equivalent of committing suicide. When human life became too horribly fraught and impossible to deal with, you could shift shapes and go and become whatever you were as an animal. For years. Sometimes decades.

Not that anyone had ever told this to Rafiel in so many words. It was just that he had talked to enough older shifters now to hear the lacunae in their stories. If you were a shifter in your hundreds, chances were you'd spent some time being an animal, somewhere, in the wilderness, or a zoo, or in the case of a very charming elephant who had been pulled in for driving on an expired license—a hundred years out of date, to be exact—in a wilderness preserve somewhere in the middle of Kansas.

Coming back from being in animal form, usually, involved some kind of epiphany or a call to return to the world by someone or something the shifter prized.

It wasn't that Rafiel didn't get it. The lion's head was so much easier to be in when the world went crazy. He could just think about shelter and food, cold and heat, and not, for instance, how to tell Mr. Milagros that Mrs. Mayor had followed her husband into the undiscovered but smelling of grilling country from which no traveler returned. And that they'd never solve the crime, because it wasn't a crime.

It wasn't like they could tell Mr. Milagros that this was the way phoenixes reproduced, though Rafiel would be willing to give up a year of salary for the privilege of seeing the chief of police react to such news.

While he thought through it, he'd located Dr. Fleming, Fleming's Pets, in the directory, and dialed. He expected an answering service, but what he got was a man saying, "Yeah?" while something like a TV played in the background.

"Dr. Fleming?"

"Uh... Yeah?"

Another long silence. "This is Rafiel Trall," Rafiel said. "I'm a Goldport police officer with the Serious Crimes unit." He heard not quite a protest, but the sound someone would make before protesting that they couldn't imagine why they were being called, and hurried.

"And a lion shifter. Do you have any way to get in touch with the zoo's shifter community?"

"A— Oh. A lion—" The man was clearly processing it slowly. "Yes. I have Aimee Morgan's number. She's probably not there, it being New Year's. But she knows how to get in touch with everyone."

"Right," Rafiel said, and conscious of the fact that any minute now the guard from the morgue could look out, or an ambulance would drive up with a fresh corpse, or something, he rapid-fire recounted an abbreviated version of what had happened.

There was less surprise than he expected.

"I know exactly what you're dealing with," Dr. Fleming said. "I mean, I knew this guy back in Araby in the fourteen—" He paused. "Never mind. I'll try to get the spider monkeys to you as soon as possible. I presume they knew Eva."

"Eva?"

"The mayor's wife," Dr. Fleming said. "And I'll come out, too. I have no idea if I can help, but I'll try."

Rafiel and Cas stood in the middle of the parking lot as snow fell on the bits of charred meat that had been Eva Phillips, and Rafiel prayed that no one would drive by.

Out of nowhere, a thought came. "Your grandmother's name isn't Helen, is it?"

Cas looked puzzled. "Elena, actually. Why?"

"You said she remembered Troy."

"No."

"But it's possible, isn't it? Like how old Menelaus happened to misplace his wife. And the whole thing with being the children of

Zeus. It would explain why you're called Castor, of all things, which shouldn't happen unless you have a twin."

"No. Polydeuces and Helen weren't wolves," Cas said. "They were born from an egg, remember?"

Rafiel didn't know that he'd ever known that, but at any rate, being born from an egg certainly didn't reassure him that they weren't shifters. It made him wonder how many of the people in mythology had been shifters.

Loki, apparently, had come by the diner a few days ago, and was a horse shifter, of all things. The way that Tom had described him, it would have been a great disappointment to all fans of the movies, too, as he was small, greasy, and wearing an old raincoat. And he'd stolen the Pearl of Heaven, for reasons known only to... Well, Loki.

And of course, the Old Sky Dragon was practically a god in Chinese mythology.

"I wonder how much of the pantheon is running around," Cas said, his brow wrinkling.

"Uh, I was just thinking the same," Rafiel said. "How much of every pantheon. Is your grandma a wolf shifter?"

"Rafiel, I'm not going to discuss this. Not right now."

Which is when all lights went out.

All of them, including the streetlights.

K YRIE NURSED THE BABY, and the nurse took him away. "We'll bring him back any time you ask," she said.

Kyrie's mom kissed her and told her the baby was beautiful.

Kyrie laughed. "He's mostly wrinkled and red," she said.

Her mom was crying. "You looked like that when we—"

Kyrie grabbed for her mom's hand and held it. "It's okay," she said. It wasn't. Or it only partly was okay. Yes, of all the places her mom and dad could have left a baby, the door of a Catholic church on Christmas Eve had been okay. Of course, she had been passed on to various foster services, and moved around a lot, which was not a manner of growing up that Kyrie would actually recommend to anyone, except...

Well, she had grown up, hadn't she? There were things in her family that no one talked about openly. She knew her grandfather had been the leader of the lion kraal, which sounded kind of neat and interesting, except when you heard things about babies eaten, or when you understood that he didn't have much use for anyone who wasn't a lion shifter. Or—

Kyrie wasn't going to think of what her sisters—three of them—might have put up with growing up. Or the fact her parents had been little more than bound slaves for most of their lives until the old horror had died.

She shook her head and clutched her mom's hand really tight.

Somewhere in the periphery, Tom was talking to her dad.

She pulled her mom really close and whispered, "Mom, the baby is a shifter."

Her mom looked at her, startled. "You are shifters, honey. Both of you," she whispered back.

Kyrie shook her head. "We were told that because we were different kinds of shifters, the baby wouldn't be a shifter. We were told he would be normal."

Her mom inhaled. It was a sharp inhale, and for a moment, Kyrie thought that she might have squeezed her mom's hand too hard. But then her mom whispered back, "You know, shifter families have been around a long time, and shifters live a long, long life. Just because you have a shifter type in your family tree, it doesn't mean you don't have others."

"Oh, but I thought—" She didn't even know why they were whispering like this, since as far as she could tell, it was only the four of them in the room.

"Pick your heartbreak, honey. Which do you prefer? He could be normal, and you could see him age and die, centuries before you. Or he could be a shifter, and you'll have to worry a bit when he becomes a teen about what kind of shifter he's going to be. And teach him to survive in the world of humans. But when he's all grown up, you guys can be friends for a long, long time."

Kyrie had never thought of that, that any normal child she and Tom had would die centuries, maybe thousands of years before them.

She opened her mouth to answer.

Which is when all lights went out.

Alarms sounded. Feet ran outside the hallway.

Kyrie's mom looked outside the window. "All the lights have gone out in the city," she said.

"Doesn't the hospital have a generator?" Tom said.

Outside there were scuffles, and screams, and alarms.

"Ms. Ormson?" Doctor Henry said from the door. "A dragon has taken your baby."

And then there were sounds from the dark that Kyrie was sure meant Doctor Henry was shifting.

She shifted.

She'd never shifted so fast, so painlessly.

One moment she was in the hospital bed. The next, she was running through the dimly-lit hallway, while doctors and nurses ran, and someone said something about life-support machines and generators. She shed the shreds of hospital gown along the way.

The Kyrie running through the hallway was the panther, huge paws padding, while she ran over and around people.

She could smell her baby and another smell, one that made her want to claw her nose out.

Through the miasma, she barely perceived her father and mother—more smell than sound or sight—somewhere behind her.

C ARS PULLED INTO THE morgue parking lot. Rafiel held his breath. He was sure the lack of lights had caused accidents, and— But the vehicles pulling in were compacts and smaller SUVs and a zoo supply van.

Out of them, in something that looked like all the skits about clown cars, a tribe came pouring out.

The spider monkeys at the Goldport zoo—about which the zoo bragged ecstatically in all their literature—were all shifters. It was possible, though Rafiel had never asked, that all the spider monkeys in all the zoos in America were shifters.

They seemed to be special in shifterdom by being able to shift from the moment they were born. In fact, he didn't know how they managed births without the caretakers knowing, unless the caretakers were in on it. In fact, this was entirely possible because the spider monkeys were somewhere between a tribe and a criminal enterprise. Maybe that was the state of all shifter clans, after all.

Despite living at the zoo, or perhaps because of it, the spider monkeys had a secret compound underneath their exhibit, where they all lived with modern conveniences. Liz and Arthur, the matriarch and patriarch of the family, directed their descendants with whispers and gestures.

In a moment, there were many dark-haired, smallish people who looked vaguely French swarming everywhere, cleaning pieces of mayor's wife from every possible surface.

Liz approached Rafiel. Just then, a small white car pulled up and Dr. Fleming climbed out. "Oh, good. You're here," he said.

"Of course," he said. He was tall man, with a neatly trimmed beard, and his blue eyes sparkled with humor behind his glasses. "This is a fascinating method of reproduction, for one. I want to know more about all of it and how it goes on."

Liz gave him a reproving look. "Poor things. They have to die to have babies. And they never get to see the babies. It's not a surprise that phoenixes are so rare. It's surprising they reproduce at all."

The gang of spider monkeys was collecting pieces into what looked like little blankets.

Liz looked pensive. "He is in there, isn't he? I mean the pieces?"

Rafiel nodded. "Presumably."

"Well, they probably won't develop when they're refrigerated, but we should get them."

Rafiel cleared his throat. "I presume there is a guard. I can't—"

"Oh. We're not asking you to. The electricity is off, see?"

"And?"

"That means that the alarm should be off, too," Liz said, and smiled. It was a very disquieting smile.

"But what are you going to do with the children?" Rafiel asked. It was one thing to dispose of a bunch of beetle larvae who would have grown up to be children, since their cycle of reproduction required them to kill people to survive. But with the phoenixes, it seemed like their reproduction was merely terrible for them and not anyone else. He was aware of groups of people going, very quietly, around to the back of the morgue.

Moments later, they started coming back, carrying armfuls of the little blankets.

"We have a large family," Liz said. "All over the country. We'll foster them out. It's important not to keep them together."

"Why?" Rafiel asked. He was thinking of Kyrie, who'd grown up in foster care, though unfortunately—or perhaps fortunately—not spider monkey foster care, She had to wait till her early twenties to meet her parents and sisters.

Liz gave him a long look. "You don't know much about phoenixes, do you?"

He sighed. "Until today, I knew absolutely nothing. I didn't even know they really existed."

Rafiel noted that Cas was talking to Arthur, and wondered if they were both talking over the same thing. Cas kept shaking his head.

"I wonder, you know," Liz said, in a tone of long suffering patience. "I wonder how bad this Ragnarök is going to be. None of you young people seem to understand much about the world of shifters. It's like every Ragnarök destroys more of the knowledge and leaves us exposed." She sighed. "The phoenixes, if all together, can be killed together. Once they're babies, I mean. And the energy release from that..." Liz sucked in air through her teeth, like someone describing a big fortune. "Well, that could blow a big hole in the shield of the world. I think that is why he told them that they could mate now, and he lied to them that it would take ten years to happen. He was planning to get all the babies. I figured that out when Eva told us what was going on. We told her we'd take the children. We'll distribute them all over the world, have no fear."

Rafiel, who hadn't even thought of having fear before, just blinked.

Snow was swirling in faster, now, and Doc Fleming was now arguing with Cas. Which is when Rafiel's phone rang.

"Well?" Mr. Milagros asked.

"We're following leads. It's difficult because we're in the dark."

"You're not supposed to be in the dar—"

"I mean, the electricity is down."

"Yeah—" Mr. Milagros paused. "No one knows why. Portable generators are having trouble working. At least cars still work."

Rafiel wasn't sure what the train of thought to that was, and wondered if Mr. Milagros knew more than he did. Liz had been offensive, but she hadn't been wrong. Despite the sense of all the lions in his mind, there was a feeling that there was a huge amount he didn't know. What he knew was the little part of the iceberg bobbing above the water, while what he didn't know was the invisible mountain upon which his whole life would flounder at any moment.

His phone buzzed, and he looked down. It was Bea, his fiancée. He picked up. "Rafiel?"

"Yes?"

"We've just got an all alarm call in our minds from Tom. Someone took their baby."

"What?"

"From the hospital. Someone took their baby. Something to do with the Pearl of Heaven."

Rafiel closed his eyes and counted to twenty. Backwards. In French. Which was particularly difficult since he didn't speak French.

And then he was getting in the SUV.

He heard Cas shout, "Not me. I don't care who gets it. Maybe some bear out there, but it won't be me."

"Surely you understand," Dr. Fleming said. "Your ancestry—"

"Rafiel, where are you going?" Cas asked.

Rafiel, already backing out, his window rolled down enough to talk, shouted. "Someone or something kidnapped Tom and Kyrie's child."

Cas stood for a moment, as though frozen, staring at Rafiel, as Rafiel turned to leave the parking lot. Then he ran up to the window. "Who— How do you know where to go?"

"I can—" Rafiel hadn't thought about it, but suddenly realized this was true. "I can feel the child's distress." And something else. Something dangerous and unclean. And cold. "I will go."

"Wait," Cas said. He was jumping in his car, while Dr. Fleming ran to his.

As Rafiel tore out of the morgue's parking lot, he realized he was being followed by a fifties vintage Cadillac and a small white compact. *It's like Noah's ark,* he thought. *Where I go, a variety of animals follow.*

At least Tom hadn't sent out a general call, Rafiel thought. The one time he had done that, the entire city had been clogged with shifted forms making their way to his call. If he did that now, in the dark, it would be interesting. And possibly lethal.

He drove for quite a while before he realized he was headed for Town Park, where the botanic gardens had been at the turn of the century. All that remained behind now were some beautiful old trees, a lot of lawn, two large lakes, a bunch of sculptures and a lot of geese, which, the way this was going, were probably going to turn out to be shifters.

K YRIE WAS RUNNING THROUGH the night. From the scent ahead, Dr. Henry was also in hot pursuit. He seemed to be a black panther, same as Kyrie and her dad. She didn't think—not precisely—as a panther, but the flicker image of thought passed through her head that indicated they were probably related somewhere not too far off.

A shadow passed over her, and she identified it as the shadow of Tom, flying, wings outstretched.

Then another, and another. She had a sense they were friends.

It was cold. Very cold. Her paws hurt as they struck the frozen sidewalk. The streetlights flickered on, then off. The roads were deserted, save for a few cars driving very slowly in the dark.

It flashed through her mind that it was probably just five or six o'clock. But that was dark in winter.

And she had to find her cub. Before something terrible happened.

TOM HADN'T SHIFTED TILL the panthers and lions had left the building. No humans had come into the room, and he figured he would be better off as a dragon. But he wasn't going to shift as Kyrie had, all of a sudden, and on impulse. He was going to shift with malice aforethought.

He wanted his child back. As much as Kyrie did, and probably more, but there was more to it than that.

He could sense the thing that had taken his baby, a dark thing, a presence like corrosive acid in the dark, shifting night. It was all somehow intertwined with ice, a graceful arc of ice. *It existed before the world and is not of the world. It spins ice that steals minds.* Tom had no idea where the words had come from. It was somewhere deep within him, the knowledge he'd acquired with the knowledge and powers pertaining to the Great Sky Dragon. He sensed that the lights going out was related to some creature and that the creature spun this... ice thing as though it were pulling all sorts of power into itself.

And Tom very much doubted that whatever it was had come in here to steal the baby. He had a feeling it had been done through thralls, maybe even dragon thralls. Had to be a dragon thrall. Dr. Henry had said a dragon had stolen the baby.

Suddenly it clicked into place that it was connected to the dragon in the diner, somehow. And he wondered if any of it had anything truly to do with the Pearl of Heaven, or if it was something quite different. Had the dragon in the diner sensed that Kyrie's water had broken and come looking for the baby? If it was a Norse dragon—in stasis for all of civilization—it might not have realized that babies weren't usually born wherever the mom happened to be anymore.

Part of him wanted to go check on the Pearl of Heaven. Another part that seemed craftier and more ancient than his current body told him that would be stupid, and exactly what they—whoever they were—wanted him to do.

He stood in the hospital room and took a deep lungful of the disinfectant-tainted air. Carefully, delicately, he reached to the minds of the dragons he knew and could trust—which, in this case, included the Great Sky Dragon—and told them what had happened. He could feel the flurry and alarm back, and he could feel the Great Sky Dragon's not-quite-promise that it would be pursued.

Along what felt like a private line came the GSD's insistence that this was a ruse to get the Pearl of Heaven. And he might be right. But what a ruse. When it came to taking a man's only son, it was bound to get his attention.

On the other hand, Tom had read history and mythology. His predicament wasn't unique.

He could feel his son, and the dark presence surrounding him. He knew where his son was being taken. And it was time to go and get him.

He folded his clothes, and rolled them into the belt pouch he wore around his middle, and which was flexible enough to stay on the dragon. He put his phone and keys on special holder bracelets.

And then he opened the window to the room, letting wind-driven snowflakes in.

He'd completely shifted when he heard someone scream behind him.

He jumped forward, stretched his wings, and headed to Town Park.

T OWN PARK WAS EERIE in the dark, with the snowfall. Rafiel parked in one of the outer parking lots.

In the dark, he could see shapes moving and was alarmed, then realized they were lions and panthers. One of them, he was sure, from scent and feel, was Kyrie.

Above there were wings.

But the thing that called his attention was the thing growing out of the middle of the lake in the center of the park. Whatever it was must have disturbed the geese, because their cries rose in the night like a cacophony of ill-tuned wind instruments.

They rose in clouds from the lake.

In the center of it... Well, it looked like a bridge, made of shiny ice. Rafiel remembered Kyrie mentioning something like it in the parking lot of the diner, created by the Norse Queen.

It was beautiful, an arch whose topmost part disappeared into the clouds, the other end not even visible.

And on it, something moved.

Looking close, Rafiel realized it was a human shape. With— Yes, it was a baby sling on his back.

He opened the door to the car and realized that he was shifting. He had just enough time to take his clothes off.

He jumped out of the car, as a lion, just in time to see Orvan the minotaur walking a few steps ahead, while at his feet an alligator slithered.

He saw Kyrie and her mother—he thought it was her mother—leaping towards the bridge, and was suddenly taken with a sense of utter wrongness.

Never having reached into anyone's mind in a rush, Rafiel wasn't sure precisely how to do it, but he willed his mind to touch the minds of all the felines present. "Don't," he commanded. Just that: "Don't." It was given with the authority of the lion kraal and strong enough to cause them to stop. He heard Kyrie's growl from where he was. She wanted her child, and he could not blame her, but... Something was very wrong. And he couldn't think in lion form.

Carefully, with difficulty, he forced himself to shift back. It hurt every one of his bones and every one of his sinews, but he forced himself to do it, and stood, shaking, to realize Orvan and Rod, the chief of bovines and the chief of alligators had also changed.

"It's a trap," Orvan said.

"Obviously," Rod agreed, in his posh British accent.

"That's what I think, too," Rafiel said. "But we can't just let them take Kyrie and Tom's baby."

"No," Rod said. "That child is one of the lynchpins."

"One of the what?" Rafiel asked.

Rod shook his head. He gave Rafiel an alligator-like grin. "I don't have the words for it. I don't have the knowledge. But important people are born in a time of Ragnarök. And he's one of them."

"Wonderful," Rafiel said. It was too cold to stand around naked, and his human brain wasn't making much more sense of it than the lion had. He wished everyone would stop speaking in riddles.

A dragon landed behind him, and in moments he heard Tom's mind-voice sounding like he was in pain. *I can't let them take my child.* And then, *We can't touch the bridge. That ice...it feels...poisonous. Deadly. But I should be able to fly up and take the baby. I should be able to—*

TOM WAS THINKING HE could do a fly-by and take the baby, perhaps with the attached human, without touching the bridge. He felt it was important not to touch the bridge, because if he did, he would become part of whatever it was that was trying to trap them all. The bridge was to the creature as a web to a spider. You'd become stuck. Mentally attached to it, via the bridge. On the other hand, if you destroyed it, it would kill you.

The human—he couldn't see who it was, which was probably for the best—crawling along its shiny surface, moved in an odd way, like he had forgotten he had bones. And yet, from the sense of him, Tom was convinced it was a dragon. And it disturbed him that he could not reach the creature's mind. There was only howling wind there, a sense of a great, unfathomable evil.

He sensed Conan about to land on the bridge, and warned him off forcefully in a mental scream, causing the smallish red dragon to try to do the equivalent of braking midair. His wings flapped the wrong way, he tumbled through the air, and landed on the lake.

And suddenly there was a voice. At first Tom had any no idea what it was saying, because it was speaking... Well, it probably wasn't even Mandarin, but some form of proto-Mandarin, a singsong language that nonetheless appeared to be ridiculously threatening.

His mind clicked, like puzzle pieces falling into place, and the words were suddenly understandable.

"You old serpent," the voice said. And Tom realized with horror it was the voice of the Great Sky Dragon. "You horror. You enemy of mankind. You don't get my son. Or my son's son."

And though part of him wanted to protest that there were quite a few more sons between himself and the Great Sky Dragon, he realized the meaning of it. He was the Great Sky Dragon's son and heir, something even more important in whatever stone-age culture the old horror had grown up in. And Tom and Tom's son were massively important...pieces of power to the whole dragon clan.

"What are you going to do?" a voice asked back. And Tom couldn't even tell if these voices were in fact auditory, or just in his head. "Touch the bridge. Go on. I dare you."

Tom flinched. He knew, as perhaps few people did, that the Great Sky Dragon was not someone you taunted. There was a feeling like a switch being thrown, and suddenly there were dragons. Many many dragons in all the bright colors of Chinese dragons, and they descended on the ice bridge.

Only they never touched it. Instead, they took up positions, everywhere but where the human carrying the baby was. Their fire hit the bridge. A smell like a million middens arose.

It didn't melt like ice. It melted like wax, dripping down in great gobs. And something, the same voice that had talked before, screamed.

"Fine," it said. "You want it? You pay the price."

There was a scream from the human clinging to the only piece still extant, as it started collapsing through the air.

Let go, Tom screamed in his mind, at the same time the Great Sky Dragon did. But the human, in thrall of whatever the other voice was, couldn't let go. He couldn't hear them. He was falling with the baby towards the freezing lake, clinging to a piece of poisonous ice, in the thrall of an old and unclean creature that the Great Sky Dragon had identified as the old enemy of mankind.

Tom flew as fast as he could, to intercept the ice, but in his way was the huge form of the Great Sky Dragon, all claws and tail. His claws flailed at Tom, his tail whipped at him, knocking him on the head.

Through the sudden darkness, Tom heard a triumphant scream. "My price. Mine to pay."

And then Tom was plunging through the sky, his conscience fading. He had a sense of hitting the water, but that was all.

R AFIEL WOULD SPEND MUCH time trying to describe it. The Great Sky Dragon had intercepted the falling piece of ice, with the human and the baby on it.

He grabbed it with all four claws, holding it in place. Something like flame came out of the ice wherever the Great Sky Dragon touched it.

The Great Sky Dragon's voice screamed something. Rafiel couldn't understand it, but he understood the gist of it, which was, "You, the red one!"

On command, Conan flew up, and grabbed the human clinging to the ice bridge remains with a claw, and pulled.

There was a sense as though they were pulling a fly from flypaper, and the human, or dragon shifter, or whatever, must have left most of his skin behind when pulled away.

Conan flew, wavily, carrying the human and the baby, whom he deposited on grass.

Meanwhile, the Great Sky Dragon held onto the ice as it flamed.

"Mine," the voice said. "Mine to control. Now you're mine, and all dragons with you."

But the Great Sky Dragon laughed, loud and insane, which shouldn't have been possible, since he was holding a big chunk of not-ice. Which burned wherever he touched it.

And then...and then he ate the ice. His mouth opened wide, wider than any mouth could open, and he engulfed the not-ice.

There was a scream from the voice. Whether pain or anger, it was impossible to tell.

And the Great Sky Dragon fell into the lake in flames.

KYRIE GOT HER BABY. The human it was strapped to was a Chinese man she vaguely recognized as the Great Sky Dragon's second-in-command. He looked like he was in shock. His hands were skinned, and he kept screaming that he hadn't meant to do it, that Nidhogg had caught him in his net, that—

Other dragons gathered around, glaring at him, but no one hurt him.

Kyrie took the baby from the pouch. He was cold, and crying, but didn't look hurt. As she held him in her arms, she felt the world was somehow right. Things were complete now.

Yes, she would be responsible for this small person, no matter what stranger form of shifter he might be, for the next eighteen years, and she'd worry and fuss over him as long as they both lived. But that was fine. That was the right shape for things. That was how it should be.

Someone put a blanket around her. She recognized him only vaguely as someone who came to the diner often.

"Dr. Fleming," he said. "I'm sorry. All I have is a horse blanket."

But she wasn't about to complain. The horse blanket was warm. Someone led her to an SUV, and she realized it was Rafiel. "Sit," Rafiel said. "You shouldn't be running around after giving birth." And it made her want to laugh, and also made her realize she was starving. But it would have to wait. "So much has happened. Where is Tom?" she asked.

"He went into the lake," Rafiel said. "Then came out. Then dove in again. After the Great Sky Dragon."

All at once, everywhere, lights came on in Goldport.

Tom did manage to find the Great Sky Dragon. What remained of him. The way he'd flamed from the inside out, you'd expect him to be all burned up, or perhaps just a skeleton with bits of flesh.

But no. He looked pretty much as he always had: a middle-aged Chinese gentleman, with neatly cut salt and pepper hair.

He was light. Tom's dragon form could lift him with his front claws without straining.

They lifted, dripping from the lake, and Tom could feel the eyes of the great assembly of Chinese dragons, some in human form, some in dragon form, follow them, as he swooped down onto a clear patch of dry winter grass and laid the Great Sky Dragon gently on it.

He looked like he was sleeping, but Tom knew he was dead. This didn't stop Tom from shifting, before he realized he was doing it, and from trying to give the old horror the kiss of life, while trying to do chest compressions for far too long.

It was all for nothing, and he knew it was as, under the blanket of falling snow, all the dragons lifted their muzzles to the sky and screamed, in unison, a cry as brittle as crystal, as cold as ice, and older than mankind.

It was the cry for a lost king. It was the lament for a lost hero who'd died to save the future.

And before the cry stopped, Tom could feel the fetters and weight of power settling on his mind and soul.

It wasn't what he wanted. It wasn't what he'd planned. But the dragons were now his responsibility. As much as his biological child, they were now his to watch over and look after. World without end.

"You bastard," he told the form of the Great Sky Dragon. "You great unredeemed bastard." He understood the rules. The Great Sky Dragon had had to eat the ice, or the ice would make him the captive of the creature—his mind whispered the name Nidhogg—and his thrall. And with the Great Sky Dragon, all the dragons, perhaps even Tom. So before the ice could corrupt him, the Great Sky Dragon had destroyed it. And himself.

Tom touched his cheek gingerly, where, in dragon form, the Great Sky Dragon's tail had dealt him a great blow. It was cut, and it would bruise. It wasn't...fair. The Great Sky Dragon had paid the price. And left Tom to pay a different one.

He reached out tiredly, and ordered the dragons to disperse, each to their own place.

But before they did, one of them brought him some kind of wrap. It was warm. It was also red silk, embroidered all over with dragons and phoenixes. And it looked like a king's mantle.

ALL THE SHIFTERS HAD poured into the diner, and taken over the annex. Other shifters, and some normal humans who were read in, like Tom's dad and Anthony, were sitting around, some of them on the floor, eating souvlaki and gyros and drinking coffee, because a lot of them had shifted into their other forms and back in the last hour. More than once.

Rafiel and Cas sat at a corner table, near the refrigerated unit with all the cakes and ice cream. Rafiel had his back comfortably wedged between the wall and the unit. He felt exhausted, though he hadn't shifted. The whole thing, the Great Sky Dragon dying, seemed surreal all by itself, without considering the hundreds of phoenix babies headed somewhere—or everywhere—through the spider monkey network.

Cas looked grim-faced, and was eating with a look like the gyros piled on his plate had done him wrong.

Nick came in, pulled over a chair, and sat next to Cas. "I told Mr. Milagros that the mayor's wife killed him, and ran off. I've... The spider monkeys say her car will be found somewhere in Denver."

"So we're pinning it on poor Eva?" Cas said. "And what about the pieces of his body disappearing?"

"She obviously took it. I gave Milagros a song and dance about a sex cult. Cannibal."

Cas moaned. "Oh, Lord. It's going to be all over the papers, isn't it?"

"Yeah. But what better way to hide a horrifying truth than with a horrifying fiction?"

Cas put his head down on the table. He mumbled something from which the word "easy" emerged.

Rafiel wanted to laugh. They had it easy. They weren't handed the leadership of a bunch of crazy lions. "So it will be taken care of?" Rafiel asked.

"Well," Nick said. He grinned, impishly. "I suspect there will be a BOLO for crazy sex cults, but we've solved a non-murder by blaming a woman beyond human justice, so we'll be okay. It's the best that can be done."

Rafiel didn't moan. But he did wish he didn't need to live a life half-buried in secrecy and lies. However, as a shifter among humans, that would never happen.

TOM SAT, HOLDING HIS baby in the annex of the diner, sitting at a table surrounded by their friends, and looked sideways at his wife.

"Why Alexander?" he asked.

She looked exhausted. She'd changed into a sweatshirt and pants, but the grey fabric made her look too pale. Dr. Henry had said he'd make it okay with the hospital before leaving, munching on a takeout box of souvlaki.

The rest of the shifters, dragon and lion, alligator, minotaur, and a rat shifter in a lab coat who'd just come off a shift at the hospital's labs, and who had heard the whole story in wonderment, ended up at the diner in the annex. Fortunately, between the lights cutting out and all the strangeness of the night, including the very odd keening sounds people reported hearing from Town Park, the diner was practically deserted. There was a couple in the corner booth, probably bewildered by the procession of people in makeshift clothes and blankets who had taken over every possible chair—and some of the floor of the annex—and by the quantities of meat they could consume.

And Tom wanted to know. "Why Alexander? It's not the name of either family. Or of anyone we know."

Kyrie smiled. Her hand, very delicately, caressed the tiny curls on her son's head. "It means defender of mankind," she said. "I think we're going to need one."

And Tom didn't really have any way to counter that, nor anything he could say against it. "All right," he said. "Alexander Ormson," he said.

"Alexander Thomas Ormson," Kyrie said. "His dad needs a mention in there."

And she smiled at him, and everything was all right.

THAT'S THE APES FOR you. And they're all apes, even those who are also dragons. Sometimes I almost think it's a pity that I have get rid of them.

There is nobility there, a flash of gold amid the dross. But must it show up just to blight all my plans?

It's just as well that I have a lot of time. And I know more than they could possibly gather.

It is a time of Ragnarök. It is my time.

www.ingramcontent.com/pod-product-compliance
Lightning Source LLC
Chambersburg PA
CBHW051249180626
46816CB00004BA/1396